Fun to LEARn

Big Daft FiSH

Written by David Cornmell · Illustrated by Woody

The story of Big Daft Fish and all the pictures in this book are original and have been specially commissioned for Tesco.

Published by
Tesco Stores Limited
Created by Brilliant Books Ltd
84-86 Regent Street
London W1B 5RR

First Published 2001
ISBN 1-84221-122-6

Text and Illustrations © 2001 Brilliant Books Ltd
Illustrations by Woody, conceived by David Cornmell
Printed by Printer Trento s.r.l., Italy
Reproduction by Colourpath, England

1 3 5 7 9 10 8 6 4 2

We live on a
very large planet
made up of land
and water, and
although we
choose to live on the
land, some creatures
make their homes
in the sea.

Under the waves are fish.
Fish with claws,
fish with jaws,
fat fish, thin fish,
fish that don't even
look like fish at all.

There are small fish
and there are
big fish.

But the biggest fish of all is Big Daft Fish. Big Daft Fish spent his days swimming with his friends.

They'd jump and dive and splash, and sometimes they'd see who could hold their breath the longest.

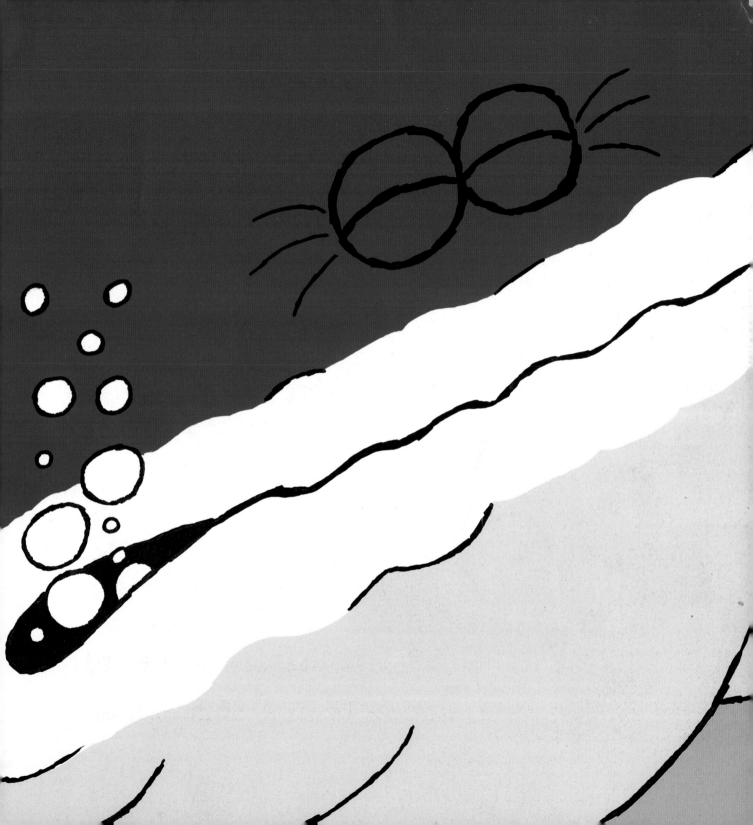

Now, Big Daft Fish could hold his breath for a very, very long time. And by the time he'd held his breath until he couldn't hold it any longer, all his friends had swum away.

Big Daft Fish was alone, so he set off in search of his friends.

He swam to cold seas.
He swam to warm seas.
In fact he swam
for so long that
he actually slept while
he was swimming.

Which wasn't very clever really because one morning he woke up to find himself on a beach.

He'd run out of sea to swim in and he was completely stuck. Big Daft Fish had to act fast.

The turtle looked up at Big Daft Fish.

Certainly.
I'll find your blubbery
friends and I'll go as
fast as my little flippers
will take me.

And with that
he was off.

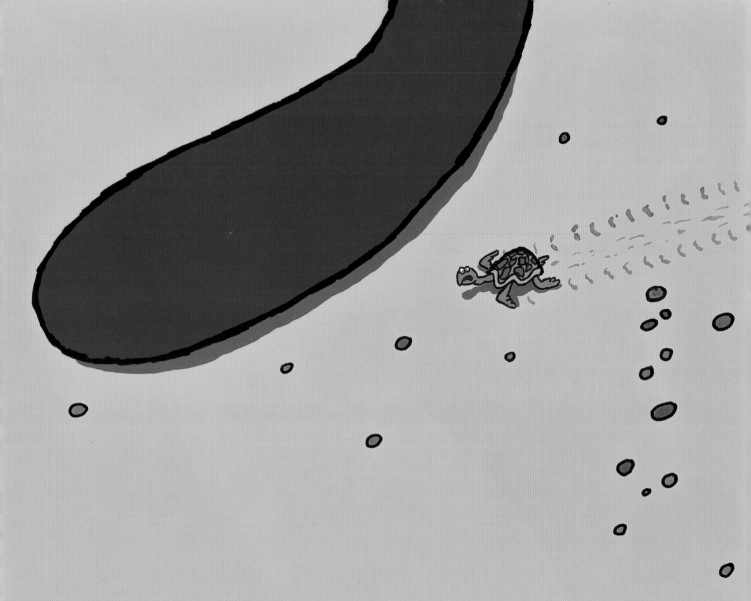

After three hours the turtle had
reached one of Big Daft Fish's fins.

By nightfall he'd reached
Big Daft Fish's tail.

And sometime
on the following Tuesday,
he eventually reached the sea.

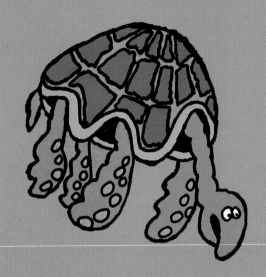

The turtle swam
until he could swim
no more, so he asked
a passing fish to help him
find Big Daft Fish's pals.

The fish swam on until he eventually found what he was looking for.

The turtle's friend thought for a moment.

Now big fish, like Big Daft Fish,
have very good hearing. So when Big Daft Fish began
to cry, his friends heard him. And soon they were
at the beach where he lay stranded.

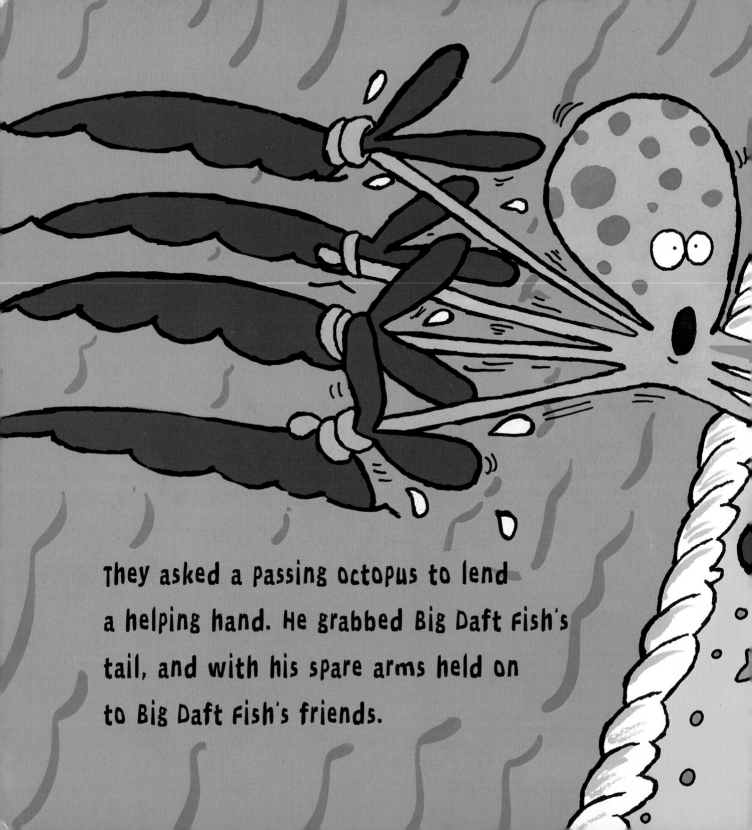

They asked a passing octopus to lend
a helping hand. He grabbed Big Daft Fish's
tail, and with his spare arms held on
to Big Daft Fish's friends.

They pulled and pulled, and slowly Big Daft Fish began to move, until eventually he was back in the sea where he belonged.

And from that moment on, he promised himself he'd never be left alone again. Because when you're big and you're daft it pays to stay among friends.